D1265854

I LOVE SPRING!

I LOVE SPRING!

Steven Kroll

illustrated by

Kathryn E. Shoemaker

Holiday House / New York

For my sister June
S. K.

Library of Congress Cataloging-in-Publication Data
Kroll, Steven.
I love spring.

SUMMARY: A young boy describes all the things that
he loves about spring.
   [1. Spring—Fiction]   I. Shoemaker, Kathryn E., ill.
II. Title.
PZ7.K9225Iac   1987   [E]   86-14844
ISBN 0-8234-0634-2

I love spring.

I love waking up in the morning and hearing the birds in the tree outside my window.

I love watching the birds build nests and the tree burst into bloom.

I love putting away my heavy, winter clothes and pulling out shirts and pants that are light and bright.

One Saturday morning in early spring, I run down the stairs and jump on my bike.

"Where are you going?" Mom asks.

"Out to meet the spring," I say.

I ride up and down my block, smelling the sweet, new grass and flowers and feeling the soft breeze on my face.

"Hello, spring, I missed you," I say, and the breeze seems to whisper back, "Missed you, Mark, missed you."

I ride past Mrs. Johnson's house so I can see her dog Zelda's brand new litter of puppies. Zelda and the puppies are in a basket on the porch. The puppies are little and warm and as soft as velvet. I touch each one very gently.

Then I ride over to the playground. My friends Judy and Jeff are swinging on the swings and climbing on the jungle gym. I climb with them, right to the top. I can see my whole neighborhood. Mr. Kerensky and Mrs. Pine are painting their houses. Everything is starting to look cheerful after the long winter's rest.

Later, when I get home, I call Judy and Jeff and ask them for lunch.

Mom and Dad make us peanut butter and jelly sandwiches, and we eat them at the kitchen table. As we're finishing our milk, Mom says, "How would you like to help in the garden this afternoon?"

Judy looks at Jeff. Jeff looks at me. I look at Mom.

"Great!" we say.

We go out into the garden with Mom and
Dad. We help them plant marigold, zinnia,
and geranium plants in the flower beds on
either side of the driveway. Then we help
them plant lettuce, pea, carrot, and cucumber
seeds in the vegetable garden.

"I can't wait to taste those crunchy
vegetables!" says Judy.

"Me either," says Jeff.

A week later, Easter comes. My parents and
I go to church, and afterwards, we have Easter
lunch at our house. Uncle John and Aunt Ellen
come, along with some cousins, and everyone
eats a lot and never stops talking.

At about the same time, Judy celebrates Passover. Her parents have a seder at their house, and Jeff and I get to go. Judy's little sister sits next to me, and we all say the prayers from the Haggadah and eat the special food that's served from a big plate in the middle of the table.

Then there's spring vacation. Jeff's dad calls. He wants to take Jeff, Judy, and me on a camping trip in the country!

We go. We climb a small mountain and look out at many other mountains. We cook hamburgers over a campfire, and then we sit and talk and watch the flames for a long time.

After that, it's my birthday. I have a party. I invite five friends. We eat ice cream and cake and drink lemonade. Judy gives me a dragon kite. Jeff gives me a book.

Then Mom and Dad take us all to a ballgame. We shout and cheer for the home team. When they score the winning run in the ninth inning, we jump up and down.

On the way home, it starts to rain. But I don't mind. I know it's good for the garden.

The rain lasts through the weekend, and Mom and Dad decide to do spring cleaning. Dad says, "Mark, please clean your room and the upstairs hall, too."

I don't like to clean my room, but when I'm through, I'm glad I helped. The house smells crisp and fresh, and everyone is happy.

Then the circus comes to town! Judy, Jeff, and I go with Judy's parents. We eat cotton candy and sit right up front. The tigers look very dangerous, but I love the family on the flying trapeze and the boys and girls riding the elephants. Just as we're leaving, a clown gives Judy a pink balloon!

A couple of weeks later, Mom and Dad and
I go to the Memorial Day parade. I watch lots
of old men and lots of younger men, too,
marching along in their uniforms. They have
all fought in our country's wars. Some of them
carry flags. There is music and people are
twirling batons, but after awhile I get sleepy,
and Mom and Dad take me home.

Lunch is an hour away, and Dad and I curl
up together in the porch swing for a nap. Dad
puts his arm around me, and I feel warm and
cozy and sleepy.
  I love spring!